Eze Goes to College

Crowder and Nzekwu

ISBN: 979-8-89693-001-3

NEO BOOKS

Contents

Chapter 1

Prince of Peace College

"Wilberforce is here to take you away, " Nurse Onwuka announced, Eze Adi, who had been sitting gloomily on the veranda of his ward watching two lizards fighting, turned with joy written all over his face towards Wilberforce Ezeilo who was standing behind Nurse Onwuka.

Even she could not compete in neatness with Wilberforce whose knife-edge creases on his shirt and shorts looked as though they were awaiting inspection by a visiting General

Although it was now three years since he had left the army, Wilberforce had lost none of his military bearing.

"Well, young Eze, the nurse tells me you are ready for discharge," he said, "Your face seems to have healed all right. And no scars.

What about your arm? How does that feel? It had better be alright as College starts tomorrow, And you must be there."

"It's much better, thank you, sir," Eze replied, lifting his right arm which was encased in plaster from his shoulder to his wrist. "I can even write a little. I've been practising for the last three days."

IIe pointed to some sheets of paper on which words were written in the hand of a child half his age.

"Well, let's be off. Say thank you to the nurse, for we must hurry to my friend, Corporal Andrew Obi's house. He's expecting us now. You'll be staying with him instead of going to the boarding house. It will be easier for you to manage there with your arm in plaster. You'll like Corporal Obi. He'll be like a father to you. He has two sons; one, whose name is Lawrence, who goes to Prince of Peace College, where you are going. The other, Philip, who is your age, is at the Dennis Memorial Grammar School (DMGS)

Nearby.

Wilberforce then turned to Nurse Onwuka and picked up Eze's haversack which she had been packing. She saw them both to the main entrance of the General Hospital. Eze was so excited about leaving that he nearly forgot to thank her for all her kindness to him during the three weeks he had been there. The terrible accident in 'Safe Journey No.

I seemed years away as he set off with Wilberforce for his new life in Onitsha. The only reminder was the plaster cast on his arm. The nurse had told him that he would have to keep it on for another three weeks as his arm had been badly fractured in three places.

Outside the hospital gate they turned right and walked along Court Road towards the magistrate's court. How good it was to be away from the smell of disinfectant, Eze thought. Even better, he would not have to eat the tasteless hospital food anymore. He didn't remember having ever been as bored as he had been those three weeks. There had been only old men in his ward who didn't seem to want to talk with him.

They came to a crossroad and turned right into Enugu Road. About 70 metres down the road. Wilberforce pointed to an archway on the other side of the road:

"There's your college," he said. Eze saw written in bold letters on the arch: **PRINCE OF PEACE COLLEGE**

A laterite road led from the arch to a large white building on a hill, flanked by two other large white blocks. His heart missed a beat with excitement, and he nearly knocked his arm against a lady going to market with a tray of oranges on her head.

"You foolish boy! Look where you're going," she cursed him.

But Eze didn't care. Here at last was what he had been striving for since he first trekked to school at Ama with his mother six years before. How he wished his mother could be here to see him now.

They turned into Ozala Road and soon came to the crossroad where it divided New Market and Awka Roads.

Wilberforce pushed a path through the crowds on Awka Road so that Eze's arm would not get knocked. Then he pointed to a large building: "That's Dennis Memorial Grammar School where Corporal Obi's son, Philip, goes."

"Why is it called: Dennis Memorial Grammar school sir? Who was Dennis? Eze asked.

Rev. T. J. Dennis?' He was sailing home on leave during the First World War when his ship was torpedoed by a German submarine. So the school, which was opened in 1925, was named in his memory."

Wilberforce took Eze's left arm and hurried him on. Soon they took a right turn down a narrow street that wound between houses of all different shapes and sizes.

Some were built in mud, some in concrete, while many were unfinished because their owners had run out of money. They came to a storey house painted bright pink with a dark green door and window shutters.

Wilberforce knocked on the door which was opened immediately by a young boy of Eze's age who must have been waiting for their arrival.

"Welcome, sir," the boy greeted Wilberforce. Then turning to Eze, he started to put out his hand but withdrew it in embarrassment when he saw the plaster cast.

"I'm Philip. Welcome. We're sharing my room together." They followed Phillip into the parlour which was dominated by a huge photograph of a man in army uniform. While Eze was looking at it, the man in the photograph entered, wearing a wrapper and a singlet.

"Welcome, back," he said, waving Wilberforce to a chair. "And is this young Eze?" he inquired.

"Who else might it be with a broken arm like that?" Wilberforce chuckled.

"Welcome home, son," Corporal Obi said to Eze. He snapped his fingers at Philip who was hovering by the door and said: "Show Eze his quarters. Then go and see your mother about food."

Philip led Eze to the back of the house where there was a small room next to the kitchen from which the aroma of food tickled Eze's nose.

In the room, two small bamboo and raffia beds were placed at either side.

"Your bed's over there,' Philip said, pointing to the one farthest from the window. "There is a locker beside it for your things. Your box is sitting on the locker. Uncle Abolitionist' brought it here." "Uncle Abolitionist?' Who's he?" Eze asked with surprise.

"Uncle Wilberforce, of course," laughed Philip. "I call him that because he was named after William Wilberforce who led the campaign to abolish the slave trade. Anyway, did he give you the keys to your box?" Eze answered with a nod.

"Good! We'll unpack your box after lunch and arrange your things. For now, come and meet Mother, my elder brother, Lawrence, and my young sister, Ebele. Then, we will get something to eat. I'm hungry."

"Not nearly so much as I am," replied Eze.

"You haven't been eating hospital food for the last three weeks. Ugh! It was awful. The cook had never tasted pepper."

Philip laughed as he looked into the kitchen. But his mother was not there. So Philip said to Eze: "Let's look for her in the parlour."

Back in the parlour, a young girl of ten was busy placing plates and cutlery on the table. Then a large smiling lady, carrying a huge bowl of steaming nsala soup entered from the pantry. Debs, corporal Obi greeted her."Have you seen our young guest - your new son Eze? Ah! Here he comes. Come and greet Mother."

"Good afternoon Ma," Eze said, stepping forward from behind Philip.

"Glory be to God." Deborah exclaimed. "I hope that arm doesn't hurt too much."

"Have you met Ebele?" Corporal Obi cut in.

"I am glad you are out of the hospital. You will recover much faster here. You will see," Mrs Obi continued.

"Now, where's Lawrence?" Corporal Obi interrupted. "In his books, I suppose. Law-rence! Lawrence!!" he called.

A few seconds later, a tall and very handsome young boy entered.

"Ah! Now the family is complete," Obi beamed. "Lawrence, this is Eze. You will be taking him to PPC until his arm is better." Lawrence gave Eze a curt greeting, hardly seeming to notice him. Eze responded shyly.

Mrs Obi who had disappeared into the pantry returned with a bowl of pounded yam, followed by Ebele carrying a basin of water. Mrs Obi set the bowl down.Come on, boys, she said, I've dished up your food in the pantry. I am sure you are all very hungry. Yours, Lawrence," she added, as the boys began to move towards the kitchen, "is in the china on the top shelf.

The food in the enamel plates on the shelf below belongs to Philip and Eze."

Meanwhile Corporal Obi ushered Wilberforce to a seat beside him and then said 'grace'.

"Aren't you coming to eat with us?"

Wilberforce called to Mrs Obi.

"I'll help Ebele tidy up the kitchen. We'll have our food there and then we will be back."

When later Wilberforce complimented her on her cooking, which Eze also assured her was the best he had ever tasted, Corporal Obi declared: "You are unfair. It is not her cooking you should compliment. It is the yam; it is the best in Onitsha. I grow them on my own farm. When young Eze's arm is better, he can come and help Philip and me on the farm. I need more hands."

Eze caught Philip's eye and Philip made a face which his father couldn't see.

About thirty minutes after they had finished the meal, Wilberforce rose:

"I must go now," he said, "if I am to get back to Ohia before nightfall. Before I go though, I want to thank you Mrs Obi, and of course, my good friend, Corporal Obi, for agreeing to take Eze into your house. I know he will be like a son to you, and that you will treat him like one."

Then he turned to Eze: "Now, young man," he said, "a lot of people have made large sacrifices in Ohia to send you to PPC. Work hard and don't disappoint them."

Eze and Philip were sent to bed early as they both had to be up at the crack of dawn to start school the next day.

Next morning at 6 o'clock they were woken by Mrs Obi. Philip helped Eze bathe and put on his clothes. Then they had breakfast with Lawrence and Ebele.

After breakfast Eze set off with Lawrence and Philip. They said goodbye to Philip at the entrance to Dennis Memorial Grammar School and continued on their way. Lawrence led Eze up the road to the main building of Prince of Peace College. Outside the entrance a large crowd of boys in white shirts and shorts, just like Eze and Lawrence, were talking excitedly. When they saw Eze, some called his name. This took Eze by surprise, for he did not know that the terrible accident of 'Safe Journey No. 1' had been reported on the front page of The Nigerian Pioneer, alongside a speech by a leading nationalist demanding that the British hand over government to Nigerians.

Lawrence helped Eze push through the crowds of boys till they reached the school notice board. There he found Eze's name on the list. "You're in Form 1A Eze. I'll take you there.

If you need me, I'm in Form IIA. But you will have to manage as much as you can by yourself. I don't have much time to look after small boys. We'll see you at the end of the day."

So saying, he led Eze to the large block to the left of the main block and pointed out the classroom of Form 1A.

In the classroom Eze met a mob of boys going from desk to desk trying to find their names which were stuck on them.

"Here is yours, Eze Adi," shouted a short little boy, "next to mine. I'm called Noah Eneli. I read all about your accident in the Pioneer. You're lucky to be alive. How do you feel now?"

Before Eze could reply, a tall white man with a mop of curly brown hair and wearing horn-rimmed spectacles entered the room.

The boys all stopped talking and stood up.

"Sit down, boys. I am your form-master.

My name is Mr Johnson. I'll be taking you for English and Latin. Now I shall call the roll to see that you are all here." What on earth is Latin?' Eze wondered.

They had never done that at Obodo Central School.

"Adi Eze" he heard his name called.

"Present, sir."

"Are you dreaming, young Adi? That's the second time I've called your name. Now pay full attention. With your arm in plaster and the difficulty you are going to have writing, you'll need to be even more attentive than the rest of the other boys."

Chapter 2
Empire Day Empire Day

Three weeks after he had started school, Eze went to the hospital to have his arm taken out of plaster. It felt wonderful to be free of the cost at last. But his arm was very weak and he was told he could not play games for another six weeks until it recovered its normal strength.

Eze watched his class football games wishing he could be on the field. Noah Eneli, his new-found friend, was a wizard on the field.

Though he was one of the smallest in the class, he had superb control of the ball. Eze could never play as well as him. Sometimes Eze would watch the Third Form games. In these, Lawrence was undoubtedly the best player. Boys said he would be captain of the school football team one day, and help give them victory over DMGS. For the past three years PPC had lost to their rivals.

On Thursday afternoon the whole school rehearsed the march-past for Empire Day.

Eze sat watching them, his feet keeping time. Mr Johnson had explained the significance, of Empire Day to the class, It was their chance to show their loyalty to their King George VI, and to the great British Empire of which Nigeria formed a part, After Mr Johnson had finished his talk and dismissed the class, Noah Eneli took Eze to one side:

"My father says the British should leave Nigeria," he whispered, "We should be allowed to govern ourselves. The Whiteman took our country by force and now we should drive him out."

Eze had never heard talk like this before and felt very confused. He didn't know what to reply.

"Don't tell anyone I said that," Noah continued. "I don't want to get into trouble with Mr Johnson. He is a nice man and wants to help us. But my father says all people should be allowed to govern themselves, It is what one of our leading nationalists said- I can't remember which one now - said in the same issue of the Pioneer in which we read about your accident."

The bell rang for the next class and Eze had no time to reply.

A week later, when Eze had all but forgotten Noah's conversation and they had just had their final rehearsal for Empire Day, Eze waited for Lawrence to come off the field so that they could go home together.

As his arm was now strong enough, he took Lawrence's books. Lawrence let him do so, but didn't speak to him. Though Eze, who worshiped Lawrence, did not know it, the older boy was embarrassed to be seen in the company of a small boy from Form I.

When they arrived home they could hear loud shouts coming from the parlour. When they entered, they saw that there were two men with Corporal Andrew. All three were talking at the same time:

"It's a disgrace," Eze heard the chubbier of the two visitors cry, "The British have outstayed their welcome. They should go now and leave us to look after our own affairs."

"Who says they were welcome in the first place? No one asked them to come, his companion shouted "Well, I certainly thought, when I went to fight for the British that I was fighting for the sake of freedom including my own.

That's what the British officers in our battalion told us. We were going to make the world safe for democracy. And now when these Zikists demand their democratic rights, what do the British do? Lock them up. They have given India their freedom.

But here they take what little we have away."

At this point Corporal Obi noticed Lawrence and Eze's presence in the room.

"Good afternoon, sirs," they both greeted.

"What is it, father?" Lawrence asked.

"What's happened?"

"The British governor has locked up all the Zikists, those young men who say Nigeria should be given its freedom now. They have put their President, H. R. Abdallah, away for two years. There will be real trouble in the country if the British go on behaving like this," Corporal Andrew told Lawrence and Eze.

"Abdallah was right when he said that he was a free citizen of Nigeria and not a subject of any foreign government. He may be in jail now. But mark my words; he and his colleagues will soon be free. Dr Azikiwe will see to that," the thin visitor almost shouted.

"Don't involve these innocents in politics or they will grow wild," said the fatter man.

"Go, have lunch boys and do your home-work."

Eze felt very confused by what he had heard. He found it difficult to think of Mr Johnson in the way Corporal Obi talked of the British. And yet he had read in history lessons how Britain was the home of democracy and free speech, and that in Britain each man had a vote. Corporal Obi was right. If the British practised this at home, why could they not do so in Nigeria?

Next morning when he arrived at class, it seemed the boys could talk of nothing else but the jail terms passed on the Zikists. All those who were day boys had heard their fathers and relations talk bitterly of what the British had done.

When Mr Johnson came into the class, they all fell silent. They did not even give him their customary greeting.

Looking very surprised, he asked:

"What is the matter with you boys? Have you forgotten your manners?"

No one answered his question.

"Well, what is it?" he asked with anger in his voice.

Still no one replied.

Mr Johnson turned to Eze, who sat in the front row as his surname began with A.

"Well, Adi, perhaps you can tell us. Or, are you dumb like the rest of them?" Eze stood up nervously, all eyes upon him:

"Well sir," he stuttered. "I suppose it's because we are all very upset about why the British have jailed the Zikists. We don't understand why the British government won't let people in our country say what they want."

At this point Mr Johnson exploded: "Politics should be of no concern to boys your age. And rabble rousers like the Zikists aren't going to help you get places in the University College, Ibadan. To make sure you understand this, you will all stay in for an hour this afternoon after the final rehearsal for the Empire Day parade is over. Now open your Latin textbooks at page 32."

After class, the boys were full of anger at Mr Johnson. Much as they liked him, he now seemed to be just like any other English-man. He didn't understand that their fathers wanted to run their own affairs. That afternoon's rehearsal for the Empire Day parade was the sloppiest yet. Eze could see many of the boys marching out of step and the band kept missing beats. What would happen on the day itself?

Empire Day dawned to a clear blue sky and a gentle breeze. When Eze got to school, it was as though the events of the past week had been forgotten. All the boys were dressed in their best uniforms and the masters had hoods and gowns on. Parents and other guests, together with a large number of townspeople, had assembled around chairs beneath a clump of shade trees near the saluting base.

The band struck up: 'God save the King' and then the boys set off marching to Lili Bolero', a tune Eze liked. How he wished he could have been there with the others proudly marching for the school.

Chapter 3
Trouble at the Mines

It was not until November 1949, when Eze had been at Prince of Peace College for nearly ten months, that his mother first came to visit him. Much as she had wanted to come before, she neither had the money for transport, nor would Wilberforce let her come. He did not want her pampering her only son, as he knew she would.

Mrs Adi and Wilberforce arrived as a delegation of two sent by the Ohia Scholarship Committee to deliver Eze's school fees to Corporal Obi.

Among Mrs Adi's personal reasons for paying the visit was, of course, her desire to learn at first hand the progress her son had made since he left the hospital. She was particularly anxious to meet her son's foster parents and see how they were looking after him. She brought with her some kola nuts and alligator pepper as presents for the Obis. As a poor struggling widow, this was the most she could afford. The delegation arrived at their destination that afternoon in heavy rain. Wilberforce was protected from drenching by his old army raincoat. Eze's mother had a conical palm leaf rain hat, which did not protect her very well.

Corporal and Mrs Obi welcomed them warmly. "What a wicked thing to do," the Corporal cried when Wilberforce introduced his companion. "Why didn't you take shelter somewhere until the rain subsided? Better still, you should have swapped rain gear."

"We are children of nature," replied Wilberforce. "We do not fear the elements."

"Must I always remind you that we left the Burmese jungle a long time ago?"

"There they go again,". Mrs Obi complained. She took Eze's mother by the hand:

"Come, let us take care of your wet clothes or you'll catch pneumonia."

When they returned to the parlour, Eze's mother had changed into the blouse and wrapper Mrs Obi lent her. Then Mrs Obi welcomed the guests formally with two kola nuts presented in a saucer. Wilberforce accepted the saucer. He took a nut in his right hand and prayed:

"Who brings kola nuts, brings life. May we live to a ripe old age? May our children be excellent students so that they may win that which we, their parents, missed? When the giant rat grows old, its young ones suckle it. May our children take good care of us after we have finished bringing them up." He broke the nut into pieces, picked one and threw it into his mouth and pocketed the unbroken nut, mumbling apologetically:

"When kola is taken home, it tells who presented it." Mrs Obi retrieved the saucer and passed the remaining pieces round before returning to her seat.

"Before we start getting our priorities wrong," Wilberforce said, dipping his hand into his trouser pocket, let us deliver a message we have for you." He brought out a thick envelope which he placed on the stool by Obi's chair:

"The Ohia Scholarship Committee has sent us to hand that over to you with its compliments."

"What is it?" Obi asked, wearing a suspicious look.

"It is Eze's school fees for two years," Wilberforce explained as Corporal Obi picked up the envelope, examined it and weighed it in his hands. "The Committee wishes you to disburse it on its behalf." Corporal Obi flung the envelope to an unsuspecting Wilberforce who managed to catch it before it could land at his feet.

"Give my best regards to the Committee," Corporal Obi told the delegation. "Tell it that we are touched by the confidence it has demonstrated in us. Tell it that we reject its offer because Eze has won a full scholarship from us, the Obis. The least we can do for a boy who is like a son to us is to educate him as we have been doing these past ten months."

Wilberforce protested vehemently.

"Ohia can offer another one or two scholarships with that money," Mrs Obi interrupted. "And, if those are not enough reasons to justify our decision, take it that this is just one small way in which we are showing appreciation for the great debt we owe you?" She was referring to the time Wilberforce saved her husband's life. Corporal Obi and Private Wilberforce as he then was, had been in the steaming jungles of that far off land for six months. Along with many thousands of other Nigerians they were helping the British fight against their Japanese enemies in the Second World

War. The day Corporal Obi nearly lost his life, he and eight riflemen were on patrol in the jungle with their British officer. As they hacked their way through the thick bamboo undergrowth, Corporal Obi, who was out in front, stumbled and twisted an ankle. He was fortunate that wilberforce, who was always very alert, heard him cry with pain. Just then, a Japanese sniper in the trees fired at Obi and missed him. Quick as a flash, Wilberforce, who was a first-class shot, picked off the sniper and the British officer quickly ordered his men into defensive positions. It proved however to be a solitary sniper who had taken advantage of Obi's incapacity.

Wilberforce knew when was defeated. He shrugged his shoulders in resignation and put the envelope back in his pocket. "How can Ohia ever thank you enough?

Eze's mother exclaimed.

"Your son is a very good boy," Obi said "You brought him up well. He is bright, intelligent and obedient. He has one problem, though. We are now in the masquerade season and he can't move about freely. We have however completed arrangements to have him initiated into the masquerade cult to-morrow."

"That's very kind of you. I never dreamed that Eze would have a father again."

"God never sleeps," Mrs Obi reminded

Eze's mother fell on her knees and touched her forehead to the floor in gratitude to God. She was returning to her seat when Lawrence and Eze came home from school. With difficulty the boys suppressed their excitement long enough to greet their elders.

"Papa," Lawrence began, "A terrible thing has happened." "Out with it," Obi ordered.

"There has been shooting at the Valley coal mines. Many men have been killed," Lawrence told his father breathlessly.

"Now, don't get overexcited. Tell your story in an orderly manner."

"We came out of the school compound this afternoon and found ourselves walking behind two constables. One asked the other if he had heard the bad news. When he said he hadn't, the first one told him that there had been trouble at the mines. A European police officer had ordered the police to fire at the miners. As a result, 21 miners were killed and over 100 wounded. The second constable asked who told him and he said that he was at the police station when the telephone message was received."

"This is terrible," Obi said. His voice had gone hoarse. "Is this the freedom, the democracy, we were drafted to fight for in Burma?" Wilberforce asked them all, angrily. "Is this why we lost our lives in foreign lands?" When no reply came, he went on: "Corporal Obi, you have more leisure than I. You read the newspaper everyday. I know that the miners had embarked on a go-slow strike action. How can that now lead to the death of so many people?"

Obi explained patiently: "For some time now, there has been unrest among the miners because they claimed that large sums of arrears due to them were being held back by the officials of the Enugu Colliery."

"Why didn't they either pay them or show them that their claim is unfounded? Why shoot them?"

"I don't know," Obi replied. "We need to have more information."

While the men debated the issue, the women and the boys retired to the pantry.

After lunch, Eze and Philip joined Lawrence in his room. Eze wanted to know what to expect at his initiation into the masquerade cult the next day.

"Do not jump the gun," Lawrence advised.

"All I can tell you is that it is a harrowing experience. But I am sure you will survive it. We both did, didn't we, Philip?"

"Of course," Philip agreed. "But can't we tell him a little? After all, that's what friends are for - to help one another."

"The initiation will lose its excitement if we tell him anything now. Besides, he's still a non-initiate. We will pay dearly if we should be caught letting him into the initiation secrets."

"But no one will ever know. I am sure Eze will not tell anyone, neither will we."

"That's all right. Come to the orange tree in the compound. Secrets are more safely discussed in the open than behind closed doors."

"Even the walls have ears," Philip commented.

They were comfortably seated on the branches of the tree when Lawrence began to speak. He told Eze that a party of initiates would fetch him when the time came and take him to the cult house. There, he would undergo tests that would prove his strength, his courage, his ability to survive, and his kindness to animals. Among the tests was a race with a black goat which he must win; climbing a tall, thin pole at the foot of which were scattered a variety of very sharp and dangerous objects which would lacerate and tear him up and leave him at the mercy of spiders who would, however, willingly patch him up if he had shown them kindness; a swim across a fast flowing river in which he would drown if he had been stealing from his mother, playing with girls, insulting his elders or doing any other bad thing; and finally a journey through an ant hole to the spirit world from which he would only return if he had been a good boy.

Philip, who had interrupted Lawrence once or twice to spice this account, said:

"You must not worry, Eze. Both of us will be there. We will help you. We will plead with the masquerades on your behalf so that no harm will come to you. What is important is that you embark on each test with a determination to win."

At the end of the initiation ceremony early on Sunday morning, Eze took the oath of secrecy.

"Come and sit here," the presiding masquerade invited Eze and he obeyed. "You have just sworn not to tell any non-initiate what you have seen and heard here tonight.

We know that many of them are very inquisitive. They will question you, they will beg you, and they will even threaten you to reveal to them what you know. In order that you do not disappoint them, you must tell them something. Now, here's what you must tell them and you must do it reluctantly.

The masquerade repeated the account which Lawrence and Philip had given of the initiation ceremony and went on to tell him more: "This way, you will satisfy them and yet not give our secrets away," he concluded.

That afternoon, Eze joined some other boys to attend a masquerade that had been invited to entertain at a funeral. Their party arrived early and began to perform. Its singing was backed by clappers, rattles, and a single drum. A sizable audience, attracted by the singing, gathered round the masquerade party.

Suddenly the audience panicked. Attracted by cries, Eze looked up and saw a very tall mass of raffia, belching smoke from its crown, approaching them rapidly. It was attended by a handful of elderly men who decked themselves with protective charms and painted their faces and limbs with white, blue and black dyes. Eze remembered how, in Ohia, mothers and even fathers,pushed their children into nearby houses, out of harm's way, when such dangerous masquerades were about. As he fled into a nearby house, he was dimly aware that his party had broken up, and even the masquerade he was attending had escaped.

Chapter 4
Riot in Onitsha

When Eze arrived at school on the Monday following the shootings it seemed the boys could talk of nothing else. A great crowd of them had gathered outside the main entrance to the school. Eze saw his friend, Noah Eneli, who was shouting loudly:

"Colonialists, quit before you kill more"

Just then the school bell rang louder than usual and the Principal came towards the boys, looking very stern in his white cassock. He glared at the boys:

"To your classes immediately," he ordered. "And, I want no trouble, or else none of you will sit your exams this December." Suddenly, the boys slouched off to their classrooms. Noah muttered under his breath to Eze that all white men were the same. They didn't care about the miners.

All they worried about was keeping Nigeria under their thumb.

When Mr Johnson came into the class he faced rows of surly faces. But this time the boys greeted him, for they were too frightened by the Principal's threat to do otherwise.

"Good morning boys," Mr Johnson replied. "Before we start work, I want you to know that I understand how upset you all are by the shootings at Enugu. And I want you to know also, how sorry I am about them. Now let us get on with the lesson." Eze could hardly concentrate on the Latin subjunctive. He felt so confused by what Mr Johnson had just said. From the way the Principal had threatened them, he thought white men just didn't care about the poor miners. But here was Mr Johnson saying that he was sorry about their death.

On Saturday, November 26th, Lawrence and Eze were sent to deliver some yams from Corporal Obi's farm to Sarkin Hausawa the head of the Hausa Community in Onitsha - a family friend residing at the Waterside. On their way home at about 3

p.m., they saw people flocking down New Market road.

"Let's go and see what's happening," Lawrence said. Eze was overjoyed to be included by Lawrence in this way and joined him in the milling crowd. The crowd came to a halt at the junction of New Market and Venn Roads. There must have been about three hundred people blocking traffic at that junction already. A man, Eze could not see, was shouting through a megaphone: "Down with the colonialists," he cried.

"They have killed our men. Soon they will kill our women and children."

An angry roar rose from the crowd:"We must have self-government now when we want it," the voice came on stronger. "Not when the British decide. They must go now."

"They must go, they must go," chanted the crowd.

"Let's go down and drive them into the River Niger," someone shouted.

"Flush them into the river and out into the Atlantic," cried another.

The shouts were picked up and echoed and re-echoed. As if with one mind, the crowd began milling slowly down New Market Road towards the waterfront. And that was where the large European companies had their stores. Eze was pulled along by the crowd and could not even turn to see where Lawrence was.

Suddenly, a detachment of police blocked the crowd that was already pelting the Compagnie Française de l'Afrique Occidentale, otherwise popularly referred to as CFAO, with stones and bits of wood lying on the side of the street and in the gutter. The noise of shattered glass attested to the damage the crowd was doing. Then, above the cries of the crowd, Eze heard & shrill police whistle and, though he tried to pull back, he found himself pushed to the front of the crowd. He saw a line of policemen armed with rifles, batons and riot shields.

Two of the policemen held a large banner which said, in English and Igbo, that if the crowd did not disperse, the police would fire on them. Then, through a megaphone, the British police officer in charge shouted:

"If you do not all go home now, I shall be forced to fire on you."

From where he stood, Eze could hear more sounds of smashed glass. He tried to turn to escape but the crowd was dense.

Others in the front tried to turn back, but those behind kept pushing them on.

The officer in charge of the police called through his megaphone:

"This is your last warning. If you do not go home at once, I shall fire."

A Nigerian police sergeant translated his order but the crowd could not disperse; it was so thick. Eze began to panic and tried to force his way back to safety, but no one would or, indeed, could give an inch.

Above the cries of the crowd, Eze heard the police officer order his men to load their rifles.

A more menacing crowd had formed to the rear of the police. Eze heard the order:

"Fire!"

A single shot rang out, sending the crowd scampering down towards Bright Street and the main market. As Eze was swept forward in a threatening move against the police by the crowd, a bugle sounded. I had hardly died down when a second order of. fire was given. Eze's ears were deafened by the delivery of shots which answered the command. A great cry went up from the crowd which at last began to give as the ones in the back turned and ran for safety.

"Hold your fire," shouted the police officer, as the crowd began to break up. Eze pushed to the side of the road into a small alleyway. He expected to see dead bodies lying on the ground but, to his surprise, there were none. The police had fired their volleys over the heads of the crowd as a warning which had indeed worked.

Eze flattened himself against a wall as he saw the police, with only raised batons and riot shields, charge down the street, hitting out at any of the rioters they caught up with.

After they had passed by without noticing him, he slipped out of the alleyway to see if he could find Lawrence. But there was no sign of him.

"Get that young boy there!" Someone roared from behind him.

He turned and saw two policemen running towards him. He scurried up the alley way, found a turning and managed to escape his pursuers. Fifteen minutes later, quite out of breath, he reached home to find corporal Obi, Deborah, Phillip and Ebele standing at the door. Where have you been? Corporal Obi asked angrily. And where is Lawrence? We've been worried to death about you both. You were expected home two hours ago."

As Eze told Corporal Obi about their adventure, the Corporal became more and more angry while Deborah began to wail loudly:

"Oh my Lawrence, they have killed him, they have killed my son."

"Quiet woman! Quiet!!" Corporal Obi barked at his wife. "One, who laments a loss one has not yet suffered, desecrates the land." Turning to Eze he said: "As for you, young man, you are going to get a thrashing you'll never forget. Both you and Lawrence.

Politics is one thing, riots are another. And young men like you have no business with either: You wait until you finish school before you mix yourselves in with grown-up affairs. Now you better get something to eat while I go out and look for Lawrence." Eze could not eat his food from thinking about the beating Corporal Obi had promised him Half an hour later, as dusk was falling, a cry went up from Philip: "Lawrence is home."

Lawrence entered the room, his shirt ripped down the back and one leg of his shorts torn. "Where did you go to Eze? I looked for you everywhere and then one of the police caught me. It was only by struggling that I got away."

At that moment, Corporal Obi came in. At first his face showed relief that Lawrence had returned safely, but then anger overtook him again:

"You should have known better than to go off with a crowd like that and taking Eze with you. I've promised him a sound thrashing.

Yours will be worse. Now both of you go into the backyard and strip while I get the cane." As Eze and Lawrence reluctantly walked towards the door leading to the yard he saw Philip smirking. He knew he would try and watch his shame, and hated him for that.

That night after the beating he could hardly turn in bed from the pain. Philip kept on asking questions about what had happened at the riot until to Eze"s relief, he heard corporal obi shout: if you don't stop talking Phillip, I'll thrash you too.

Chapter 5

Christmas Carols

The first Sunday after Eze arrived at the Obis, he accompanied them to their Church.

He joined Corporal and Mrs Obi in their pew while Lawrence, Philip and Ebele went away to robe in the vestry, for all three were in the choir. Eze was very impressed by the long procession of choristers and clergy which marched solemnly along the centre aisle. The church at Obodo never put on such a magnificent show. As the procession passed by Eze's pew singing lustily, he smiled at the Obi children who looked angelic in their purple robes trimmed with white.

After the service, Philip introduced Eze to the choirmaster:

"Welcome to Emmanuel Church," the choirmaster said. "Did you enjoy our service?" "Very much, sir," Eze replied promptly. "I love the singing of the choir."

"Would you like to join it?" "Let's first make sure he does not croak,sir," Philip advised.

"Would you, Eze?" the choirmaster asked again."I'd love to, sir."

"Philip, you bring him with you to tomorrow's choir practice."

The Emmanuel Church choir had begun preparations for the year's Christmas carol during the first week of Advent. Soon, the number of choristers doubled. Irregular members now turned up regularly at practice for no one really wanted to be left out of the biggest annual event in the life of the choir.

Choristers looked forward to it. For the younger as well as the older members, it was an occasion of great joy. It offered them an opportunity to parade their knowledge of songs, beautiful songs; to display the quality of their voices by singing without the organ and in the open air. It was an exciting experience to leave home and wander round the city all night. And this was something Eze and Philip would never otherwise have been allowed to do. heavy in the air. The carols had been perfected. There was a repertoire of thirty songs. Letters were prepared and were hand-delivered by the younger choristers to chiefs and elders and very important per-sonalities, irrespective of whether they were Christians or not, informing them of the choir's intention to bring to them glad tidings of great joy, between the hours of 9 p.m. on 24th December and 5 a.m. on 25th December.

On Christmas Eve, Eze and the Obi children assembled with the other choristers promptly at 7 p.m. The pastor addressed them and gave them a feast of rice, served with large chunks of meat and soft drinks.

At 8:30 p.m., after this hearty dinner, the choir lined up in front of the parsonage and opened the night's programme with:

'O Come, O Come, Emmanuel.

Next it sang:

'Silent Night'

It wished the pastor and his household a Merry Christmas and a Happy New Year with: 'God Bless The Master of This House'. The singing of carols had begun. The choir trooped out of the parsonage and the mission compound and went methodically from village to village, from house to house, bringing to its audience the good news of Christ's birth. The night was dark, but this did not deter music lovers from trailing the choir as it moved from one venue to another. The choir was aided in its performance by four Aladdin lamps which were borne aloft by four tall choristers.

When covering long distances between two stops, the choir sang some of their very rhythmic songs which helped its members shuffle, march or dance along. These songs kept them from falling asleep or feeling tired. At each stop, the choir sang two or three pieces, rendering them as if at a singing competition. At each stop, it received presents of money, goats, chicken, drinks, biscuits, sweets, cakes, sandwiches or a combination of these.

It was not until 5 O'clock on Christmas morning that the choir finally arrived at the residence of the leader of the church committee. His large compound was brightly lit. His entire household was awake, as if they had kept vigil waiting for a very august visitor.

"This is where we end our carol singing every year," Philip whispered to Eze, as they went through the gate. "We will soon come to the part we love most."

A tenor soloist intoned a tune, a short and brisk one. The choir broke into harmony in its response. Their host, with a double-barreled gun in his hand, led his guests out of the sitting-room into the morning air and fired two shots to bid the choir welcome.

As if the shots were a challenge to it, the choir broke into one of its most melodious carols. It followed it in quick succession with four others. At the end of the fifth carol, the choirmaster turned to the audience and wished everyone in it a merry Christmas.

While their host fired some more shots in appreciation of the choir's performance, some servants were busy bringing out refreshments for the choristers.

In all, there were six four-gallon kegs of palm wine and two cartons of beer for the older members of the choir, a large pot of specially prepared goat meat, one giant tray of sliced bread, some soft drinks for the young choristers and biscuits and tea. In addition to these, their host gave the choirmaster a bottle of whisky and the choir, ten pounds sterling. At the end of one hour of feasting, the choir sang a couple of songs before it took leave of the household. About one hundred yards from the church leader's house, the choir dispersed, but not before the choirmaster had reminded the choristers that they were expected to perform at the 10 a.m. church service and hoped that they would all be punctual.

Eze travelled home to Ohia a couple of days after Christmas to spend the rest of his holidays with his mother. He received a great but informal reception on his arrival.

Women flocked to his mother's house to welcome him. Children came to catch a glimpse of this newcomer from far away Onitsha. The men refused to be outdone by the women on this occasion. They all came

Eze's uncles, Iwe and Agu; Bosah, the short, thickset man with a broad chest and muscular arms: Achike, the wrestler of great local fame; Uka, the native doctor and fortune teller; Aso, the very tall, thin man who looked as though he might break in two. Eze greeted them all. He observed very little change in any of them. They still seemed the same as he had left them a year ago.

For Eze, two men were conspicuously absent. One was Wilberforce who had travelled to Lagos. The other was an old Chike. Eze asked his mother about him and learned that he had not been well of late. As he left the house to visit the old man, Eze saw him entering the compound and ran to him:

"Why didn't you send for me, Chief?" Eze said as gently as he could, "to run your errands. I hear you are very sick. You shouldn't strain yourself, you know."

The old man peered into Eze's face and a smile wrinkled his own face the more. How he had aged, Eze thought.

"Welcome home, my son," old Chike said, in a trembling voice. "I have no errands. I have only come to set eyes on you before I die."

"Don't say such things, Chief." "Take me to the house and offer me a seat. Don't make me feel like I am not wanted." He shuffled towards the house, closely attended by Eze.

"Why must I not say such things, eh?" he asked, halfway to the house. "No one in this village has a better claim to death than I have. I have lived my life fully. Now I am an old man, the oldest in these parts. Besides, I am a very sick old man. What use am I to anybody? Son, it is time to go home, before I become too much of a burden to anybody.

I feel it in my bones. It could be now, tonight or in a few days' time."

Eze urged him into the house and offered him a seat. When he was comfortably seated, he said to Eze's mother:

"Our son has come home, eh? That's good.

Cook him delicious bitter leaf soup tonight, eh?"

"I'm already preparing to do so?"

"That's good. Son, did you pass?"

"Yes, though I didn't do as well as I expected."

"Never mind; you will do better. And how are your foster parents? I hear they have two boys and a girl of their own." "You heard right. They are quite well and said I should greet all my people."

"That's good... Now that I have seen you, I must go and rest or Uka will be angry with me. Always, it is: You must not eat this, you must not eat that, yet his filthy potions have no effect. I am dying of hunger."

"Shall I bring you some of my bitter leaf soup tonight?" The old man rose and shuffled through the door. Eze walked beside him in silence until they came to the edge of the compound.

"Yes," old Chike said, "bring me some soup."

"I'll see you later, Chief."

Eze had only been in the village for two days, when it dawned on him that his uncle, Iwe, was proving too friendly for the comfort of himself and his mother. He was always calling at the house or sending for Eze to run errands for him. Wasn't this the same man who squandered my father's wealth in a lavish funeral rite:? Eze thought bitterly. Wasn't it he who seized the morey Ulu's husband presented to us? What does he want with us now? That night, his mother supplied answers to these questions that so worried him. They were eating dinner when she spoke:

"Have you noticed how Iwe suddenly has become very friendly?"

"Yes Mama. But I don't understand it."

"Iwe is a bad man. He knows we are on our guard. Now he wants us to believe that he is a friend, so that we will lower our guard and give him an opportunity to strike at us.

You just watch your step. Don't eat anything he offers you. There is no antidote for any poison that gets past the throat."

Next morning, Eze woke up wishing he had not come home. He was suddenly disenchanted with the village. Except for the time he spent at Ama everyday with Mr Okafor and other friends, and the evenings he sat by old Chike, listening to local history and words of advice, he found life in the village boring.

The children of Ohia were now finding Eze very stand-offish. They did not like his superior ways. Rumours of this reached his mother on New Year's Eve and she was very angry with him:

How dare you antagonize those whose parents made it possible for you to go to school? You must not show contempt for their children because they have not had your good fortune. Right from this moment you must show them gratitude. Leave evil to those who sow it, for nobody ever planted yams and harvested maize. And if you don't heed my warning, I'll report you to Wilberforce and your foster parents at Onitsha."

She had just finished her threat when a piercing cry shattered the quiet of the village.

Eze and his mother ran out into the night to find out what was happening. Silhouettes of able-bodied men flashed past where they stood in the direction of the cry.

After a while, they sauntered back. Only one of them stopped long enough to tell them that old Chike had passed away.

Eze and his mother spent a good part of the night at Chike's place, consoling, as best as they could, his youngest daughter who had nursed him until his death. Old Chike was buried the next evening. Everyone appeared to rejoice that he had 'gone home' at a ripe old age. But Eze was very sad at the old man's passing. Despite the great differences in their ages, he had been a true friend. At last the funeral ceremonies ended and Eze, feeling that the village held no more attraction for him, began to get ready to return to Onitsha and the Prince of Peace College.

The night before he travelled, his sister, Ulu came home from Enugu, where her husband was working as a clerk with the United African Company (UAC). She and Eze embraced lightly when she entered the house.

"Welcome, Ulu," Eze greeted her with a broad smile.

"I am glad I came. When did I see you last..? Ah! Yes, at the hospital. You looked like the image of death the day I visited you and I cried for fear of losing you. How you have grown! Is your arm completely healed now?"

"Yes, it will be some time though, before I can do any really hard work with it."

"How was school?"

"Fine."

"And your foster parents? Are they good people?" "They are the very best of people."

"Aren't you lucky?"

"See who's talking about luck. You have a doting husband. You are heavy with a child.

And see how well pregnancy becomes you..!

Your baby had better be a boy. That's the only tap root bay you can develop in your husband's home.

"Talk about things that concern your age, little boy. Where is mother?"

"She is just returning from the stream." Ulu embraced her mother as she crossed

the threshold.

"You gave no notice of your visit," her mother said, a frown on her face. "I hope you and your husband have no problems."

"Mama!" Ulu exclaimed in mock surprise; "you elderly women are all the same. No, we have no problems. My husband only sent me to tell you that he has been transferred to Kano and that we will travel there next week. He also asked me to bring you your food allowance for two months. It is not likely that you will hear from us before we settle down in our new station. And that may be weeks or even months." "May your husband not be the job-seeker who shies away from work? What is important is that wherever a child may be it wakes up with each sunrise. May God guard and guide you both... And you, Eze," Mrs Adi said quickly, in case her son felt left out.

Then she turned to her daughter "I hear foodstuffs are cheap in Kano. You'll be able to save a lot of money."

"They're not as cheap as they used to be." While they talked, Eze slipped away and paid a farewell visit to old Chike's grave.

Standing with his hands clasped across his chest, and his head bowed, he wished the old man well in the land of spirits, begged him to take care of the village and help thwart the evil plans of his wicked relations.

Next morning, as he was about to set out for Ama on his way to Onitsha, his sister made him a promise:

"If you do well at school, Eze," she had said, "I'll arrange for you to spend your next Christmas with us in Kano."

Chapter 6

A Snake on the Farm

The first rains fell late in March to herald the farming season. Eze, Lawrence and Philip went with Corporal Obi and the farmhands he had hired to the farm at weekends. Eze was assigned light jobs while the others hoed the ground, which they had previously cleared and burnt, into mounds.

When the mounds were ready, yams were planted on them and maize in the furrows surrounding them.

Each time the boys helped on the farm, they would return home in the evening with bundles of faggots. Wilberforce who had started trading between Onitsha and Ohia was now a regular visitor to the house, so they were not surprised to see him when they came home from the farm one evening.

He was sitting and discussing animatedly with Corporal Obi over a keg of palm wine:

"All we non-Onitsha Ibo are saying," he told Obi, "is that those of us who live here, work here, trade here and pay our taxes on the Council. Whether our population is on the Council. Whether our population has outgrown yours is immaterial, All we are saying is that representation on the Council should be on the basis of taxation. It is our taxes that keep Onitsha going, so we should have a say in the disbursement of the revenue we generate. After all, that is democracy."

"But what you are asking," Corporal Obi said in reply, "is that you become the banana that swamped the plantain. You want to come here into our homes and take us over. Would you allow someone else to do it in your village? And your claim to paying more taxes is just talk. Most of you don't see the wisdom in mending the thatch that shelters them, so they evade paying."

"This argument could break up their friendship if it goes on much longer," Eze remarked.

Lawrence laughed: "These two," he said, "have learnt to argue and shout, without bitterness. Their arguments do not degenerate, like those you have with Philip, into quarrels." The rains had now become steadier. A carpet of weeds covered the dark brown earth like lichen on raffia palm. The carpet was as lush as the surrounding bush which hemmed it in on all sides. The boys joined in weeding the farm to protect the tender yam shoots whose tendrils clung to thin poles stuck into the mounds to guide them.

They were weeding one Saturday afternoon when Philip called out:

"You take to weeding like a fish takes to water,

"Why don't you stop talking for once and save your energy for clearing your lot?"

"I am not a farm hand... Will you help me finish off my lot, Eze...? I'll give you a piece of meat at dinner tonight."

"Don't insult me, Philip." "Only gorillas and chimpanzees get as easily irritated as you do."

"That's enough. One more insult from you and I will teach you to respect me."

"All right, I'm sorry. I forgot that fifteen months is only long enough for one to wear a thin veneer of civilization."

Eze dropped his hoe and matchet and bounded over mounds towards Philip who fled, carrying his own matchet.

"Stop it both of you!" shouted Lawrence from where he was working some distance away.

Philip wove his way between mounds, towards the edge of the farm. About two metres to a clump of leaves on the edge of the farm, he staggered and fell.

"I can't see. I can't see," he cried over and over again.

Lawrence and Eze rushed to him. While Lawrence was asking what had happened to him, Eze bent down and pulled Philip's hand away from his face. One look was enough. He picked up Philip's matchet, studied the direction in which he had been moving when he fell and cautiously approached the clump of leaves, his matchet hand raised high above his head. As he came close, a spitting cobra darted out of the clump past him. Eze twisted himself to the right, the matchet in his hand flashing down as he did so. Fast as the cobra was, Eze moved faster.

His single blow severed the cobra's head from its wiggling body. Lawrence was very agitated. He did not know what to do as Philip continued to moan.

"I'll put our tools away," Eze told him. "We must take Philip home as fast as we can." They lifted Philip up and took turns at carrying him astride on their back. In the vil-lage, they were relieved by other boys who helped them to get Philip to the hospital.

Twenty-four hours after he was admitted for treatment, Philip was certified all right and was discharged.

"I hope you've learnt your lesson," Lawrence told him when he came home. "Go and apologize to Eze. And thank him because he saved your eyes."

Chapter 7
Ofala Festival

One evening in October, Corporal Obi gave Philip and Eze permission to go to the cinema to see the new film of Julius Caesar. It was being shown at the Alhambra open-air cinema along Old Market Road. The two boys were particularly anxious to see it as this Shakespearean play was one of their set books for English literature that year. Unfortunately for them, many hundreds of school children in Onitsha were also studying Julius Caesar. And even though they set off early, there was a long queue and they only just got seats.

Long before the lights dimmed at 8:50 and again at 8:55 p.m. as first and final warning to all that the film was about to begin, the theatre was full. The crowd outside made so much noise, in their effort to get in, that it was impossible for anyone inside to hold a conversation in normal tones with those around him.

The theatre lights went off at exactly p.m. Julius Caesar was preceded by twenty minutes of newsreel and advertisements.

The film itself ran for two hours before the theatre doors opened to disgorge its audience onto Old Market Road. Almost half the members of the cinema audience turned left and walked in the direction of the Inland Town, commenting on the film as they went.

Philip and Eze were about 30 metres from the junction of Old and New Market Road when those ahead of them stampeded.

"Don't panic," Philip whispered urgently, grabbing his companion's arms. "Let's see what the problem or source of danger is before we make a move," he warned.

As they stood, they could hear loud shouts:

"Get inside," a voice commanded.

"But I don't want a ride."

"Don't let me get rough with you. Get in-side."

"Look, my friend. I did not pay for a ride.

So I won't get inside."

"You pay, you don't pay, just get inside quietly. how can I go for a ride I didn't pay for?" Just then a powerful torchlight flashed from behind the two boys. Its beam revealed the tail of a police van parked in a side road with two policemen trying to force a struggling man into it. It also revealed a policeman creeping up on the two boys who immediately turned and fled. But it was Eze's unlucky night. Before he took two steps, a hand closed around his left arm in a vice-like grip.

"Why are you running away, young man?

What have you done wrong?" his assailant asked.

"Why were you creeping up on us like a thief?"

"Don't insult me. I am an officer of the law."

"What have l done?"

"It is not what you have done as much as what you have not done."

"You are hurting my arm."

"Never mind. Where is your light?"

"What light?"

"It is an offence to walk about after 10 o'clock at night without a bush-lamp, torchlight or even clay oil lamp. I see you don't have any."

"But we were returning from the cinema..."

"Along a public road, after 10 o'clock in the night, and without light? That's an of-fence. I will arrest you."

"Please, sir."

"Ah! So, I am now: Sir? I am no longer a sneaking thief, eh? If you force me, I will add another charge; that of resisting arrest. So, come quietly and take your medicine."

"Where are you taking me to?"

"I am taking you to the van over there, of course; for a free ride to the police station." Philip had hidden underneath a carpenter's work bench nearby and heard it all.

He remained under the bench until he recognized a group that had a bush-lamp and joined it.

Poor Eze spent the night at the police station. Luckily for him, the cells were full, so he and many students, who were arrested in the police raid on cinema-goers, were left behind the counter.

Immediately he got home, Philip told Corporal Obi what had happened. Straightway he set off for the police station to get Eze freed. But when he arrived there he found a tall policeman blocking the entrance to the station. Along with several other distressed parents, he was told to come back in the morning.

Meanwhile Eze and the other students who had been caught by the police had a sleepless night. Their main topic of discussion was when they would be freed.

"What if they keep us here all tomorrow?

We shall miss the Ofala Festival," one boy said.

"That would be terrible," the others said, almost in unison.

Eze was really upset at this thought. Lawrence and Philip had told him so much about this great Onitsha festival. Last year he had missed it because he had been in bed with malaria at the time. Now this year it seemed he might miss it again.

Ofala, Lawrence had told him, commemorated the time Onitsha people first ate yam. There had been a great famine in days gone by. In their search for food, people tried eating anything. At last they tried yam, which up till then they had believed was poisonous.To test it out they asked the smallest kindred group among them to try out the yam first, following a set course - roast yam treated with nn'edi leaves, followed at lunch time by a meal of pounded yam served with nsala soup.

Each meal was accompanied by prayers, incantations and offerings to the gods and ancestral spirits to win their support.

Kindred after kindred ate yam without fatal result. This called for a celebration, one in which the Obi, the King of Onitsha, rejoiced with his subjects at the discovery of yam as a valuable source of food supply.

As Eze was thinking about the festival he seemed sure to miss, a police sergeant came in:

"All right, you students; you can go home now; it is dawn. But don't let me catch you on the road again at night without a light. Or, you won't see the sky for several days."

Eze got home to find Lawrence and Philip taking their bath. The two boys commiserated with him. Tired as he was, he joined them so that he would not miss any part of the festival. Lawrence was telling Philip how magnificent the day would be. But Eze had always heard it said that one, who kills a snake when no one else is around, calls it a boa-constrictor. So, he kept an open mind until he had seen the celebrations himself.

At nine o'clock, when everyone in the house was dressed, three cannon shots boomed out across the town. In the palace they were telling the Obi's subjects that the great day had at last come.

Again at noon the cannon shots boomed out from the palace. This time they were a signal for everyone to get ready for the cel-ebrations. At three in the afternoon, another series of shots was fired. These invited the people to come to the palace to celebrate Ofala.

Philip and Eze ran all the way to the Obi's palace because they wanted to secure vantage positions that would give them an undisturbed view. When they arrived, Philip selected a tree behind the palm leaf sheds that were constructed along one side of the palace square to provide shade for very impor-tant personalities. They climbed the tree and settled themselves comfortably on a stout branch and waited. Soon spectators thronged the square.

"They say that in the past, men entered the palace square by one gate and women by another," Philip told Eze. "Men and women were not allowed to mingle in the old days."

The spectators were dressed in their best clothes which were of many different materials, patterns, cuts and colours. Some sat in the shed, others stood in the shade of overhanging leafy branches, and still others joined Philip and Eze on their porches for an undisturbed view.

"In the past," Philip said, "Otumoye Lake supplied people with dresses to attend Ofala, on the condition that the clothes or their rags must be returned."

"How can a body of water give people clothes?" Eze asked suspiciously.

"It is no ordinary lake. That's why."

"Why doesn't it give them clothes these days?" Eze sneered.

"They say that one greedy woman failed to return what she took and that stopped all favours from the lake."

"Hm," Eze snorted. "The stories you do

"If you don't believe me, ask my father when we get back home."

"And make a fool of myself?"

The square was already full of activity.

Drums were beating, men dancing and women singing. Female relations of the Obi gorgeously attired in expensive clothes and gold and coral trinkets paraded up and down the arena. They sang and danced traditional pieces in honour of the Obi, their voices rising high above the din which filled the air.

"Something appears to be burning over there," Eze remarked, pointing to wisps of smoke twisting lazily into the air.

"It is the rainmaker trying to scatter the gathering clouds," Philip explained.

The sound of bands performing in the distance grew louder as it closed in on all sides.

Philip explained that each band was escorting a member of the Ndichie Ume or red cap chiefs to the palace grounds. Soon the first of them arrived. The others arrived after him in quick succession. Each one of them was closely attended, as he entered the square, by his retinue of relatives and a band. He danced around the square to the rhythm of his band and then to that of the royal drums before he finally took his seat.

Drumming and dancing continued until suddenly they stopped. Eze noticed that the Onowu, the prime minister in Onitsha traditional government, was now leading all the Ndichie to the entrance to the Obi's apart-ment.

"They are going to receive the Obi and usher him into the arena," Philip explained.

All eyes were glued to the entrance and the assembly of dignitaries now blocking it.

Then a full-throated cheer went up as people sighted the Obi. The Ndichie made way for him and a wild cheer ran through the crowd as he came into full view. Then Eze saw what he thought to be an ljele masquerade - the largest and most beautiful of Ibo masquerades - towering above the attendant Ndichie, dignified, majestic and attrac-tive.

As quickly as the cheer had risen, it quickly subsided. It was then that Eze realized that it was not a masquerade but the Obi himself. As he moved forward, the Obi was flanked on either side by two boys in embroidered signal-red gowns and caps, each presenting a shining brass sword. Attended by a train of Ndichie, Agbalanze and his relatives, he went round a third of the arena in an anti-clockwise direction. The processional chant, rendered in full throated male voices, said:

"The king! The king!

Behold the king. Behold the king.'

The Obi stopped now and again to salute the shrines which lined his course. They were said to be indispensable to a prosperous reign and good government. As the Obi approached the place where the royal band was waiting to strike up a rhythm for h n, Eze got his first full and close view of him.

He saw a tall and well-built man. He wore a sleeveless jumper of brown velvet with dark spots. The jumper was fringed at the waistline with strips of the same material that descended to his ankles. His trousers were of blue and white striped velvet. Round his ankles were tied strings of tiny brass bells which jingled as he walked.

His bare arms were circled with brass armlets. He carried a brass state sword in his right hand and a horse tail, reputed to protect him from evil machinations, in his left. Crowning all these was a seventy centimetre high hat which was created with multi-coloured ostrich plumes. Beneath its wide brim, the Obi's fiery eyes were alert and watchful, for, though a joyful occasion, Ofala afforded some of the opportunity to test his magical powers.

The band was already performing when he was some three metres away from it. He danced towards it to its rhythm, signalled it to stop and retired to a specially built pavilion, where the Ndichie, in order of seniority, paid him obeisance.

The Obi emerged from his pavilion and retired to it on two more occasions. Each time the drumming and singing resumed all over the square the moment the Obi retired, ceased the moment he came out of the pavilion. Each time, closely attended by the Ndichie, Agbalanze and his relatives, he paraded the arena, saluting the shrines as he went; each time he added another one-third of the arena to that previously covered; each time he did the royal dance before retiring.

The third retirement was to his apartment and marked the end of the celebrations that day. Eze and Philip joined the retinue of the Ndichie Ume from Philip's kindred on their way home.

The Ofala Festival was, for Eze, the high point of an exciting and happy year. His work had gone well. But even better, he had begun to make his mark as a sportsman.

He found that he could run faster than any boy in his year. And he had done well, especially in the middle distances. Corporal Obi was impressed by this development.

But he was even more gratified when Eze brought home the result of the year's promotion examination. Eze had come very near the top of his class. asked Eze what his plans were for the holi-days.

"My sister said I could spend it in Kano if I passed my promotion examination," he replied. "But she has not sent my transport fare."

"Never mind. Do you have their address in Kano?"

"Yes, sir."

"Then you have no problem. Once you've been home to your mother, you'll go to Enugu by lorry and catch a train to Kano.

Don't look lost already. Students in much lower classes do the journey, all on their own, every holiday. I'm sure you'll even run into some of your classmates on the train."

"It's just that Kano is so far away and I do not speak Hausa."

Rubbish! You speak Ibo and English. That's more than enough languages to get you to Kano even on foot. The trouble with you is that you lack the spirit of adventure that characterizes boys your age."

"We must send a telegram to your brother-in-law to tell him when you are arriving, so that he can meet you at the Kano railway station."

Chapter 8
Kano

Eze set off for Enugu by lorry from Ohia. Now that the village was linked with Obodo by a dirt road, twice a week a lorry came to collect passengers and produce. Eze almost didn't want to go when he saw that the lorry was called: 'Safe Journey No. 4' and was relieved when they arrived without mishap at Obodo. There he caught another lorry called: 'God's Time Is The Best'. They covered the distance between Obodo and Ngwo, passing through Abagana, Awka, Ugwueba, Oji, and Udi, in one hour and fifty minutes. Soon after leaving Ngwo, they were wending their way down the steep slopes of Milliken Hill.

Eze had never been to Enugu before and he marvelled at the beauty of its setting. All around it rose great hills, dotted on the lower slopes with the miner's houses.

When at last they reached the Enugu lorry park, Eze asked the driver the way to

the station and trekked there with his box on his head. He had to queue for nearly half-an-hour for his ticket. When finally he got on to the train, he could not find a seat, so he had to sit on his box in the corridor.

At last the whistle went and the train snaked out of Enugu station, hooting and announcing proudly that it was on its way to the North. Eze stood watching the scenery pass by, when re felt a tap on his shoulder.

He looked round to see a face he could not quite place:

"Aren't you Eze Adi who lives in Lawrence Obi's house? I've seen you running the 440 yard race. You're doing well. You'll be champion if you keep it up... I'm Ali Bichi. I'm in the same class as Lawrence. What are you doing on the train?"

"I'm going to Kano to stay with my sister for Christmas."

"That's good; Kano's my home. I'm off to stay with my grand-parents, for my father is a cattle trader in Onitsha. When you get to Kano, you will come and see us. I have a younger brother, Adamu, who is the same age as you. He'll be happy to show you around the city."

Eze wanted to ask the older boy questions, but Ali said he had to go and join some friends in another coach.

The journey seemed endless. Eze dozed fitfully, but it was impossible to sleep in the crowded corridor. On one occasion he did manage to get to sleep, but he was awakened by shrill cries of: Bredi, Bredi. The train had come to a halt at Makurdi station and, all up and down the platform, little girls were selling bread and tins of sardines to passengers. Eze bought himself a loaf for three pence and opened the tin of sardines his mother had given him. Later, he bought a cup of water for half a penny.

After nearly an hour in Makurdi station, waiting for the down-limited train to pass, Eze's train eased itself out of the station.

Soon it was dawn and the sun rose on beautiful hills. Eze refreshed himself by leaning out of the window and letting the air rush across his cheeks. At one point the train almost formed a circle as it wound round a steep hill; so from the last coach of the train you could clearly see the engine and all the other coaches. The train passed villages with huts built in a style Eze had hills behind and entered flat country with only the occasional granite rock breaking the skyline.

Most of the land was under cultivation and was dotted with neat little villages with houses with flat roofs. In some of the villages, houses were painted with beautiful patterns. Eze felt a tap on his shoulder.

"Well, here we are in my country," said Ali. "This is Hausaland. We'll soon be in Zaria. Then it's only two hours to Kano. I'll call for you when we're about to arrive."

"Thanks," said Eze as the older boy went back to his carriage. Just after he had left, there was a loud shriek not far behind Eze.

"Thief, thief. Yeh! My money has all gone." Eze saw a large woman with tears running down her face, beating her breast.

"Oh! My money: £100. Who has stolen it?" All the passengers in the compartment looked very embarrassed and hastened to deny any knowledge of her loss.

Suddenly the woman pointed at Eze.

"That boy there. He's been outside here since we left Enugu. I'm sure he must have sneaked right up to me during the night. Search him. Search him."

Eze was horrified by the accusation. Before he could protest, one of the passengers in the compartment, a huge bearded man who smelt of stale tobacco, seized him roughly and though he struggled, stripped off his clothes and went through his pock-ets. Eze stood there, angry and shamed, in his underpants, shouting that he knew nothing about the woman's money.

The man took no notice and, having satisfied himself that Eze had only three shillings in his pockets, took his key and opened his box. He scattered all Eze's clothes on the floor as he searched for the missing money. Then he turned to the woman:

"It's not here. The boy doesn't have your money. You should be more careful about accusing people of being thieves."

He turned to Eze who had struggled back into his clothes and was now packing his box:

"Sorry young man. Here, have this for your trouble." He handed Eze a five-shilling note.

Eze refused it, but the man would hear nothing of it.

"You have been falsely accused and you deserve recompense. If this woman had any money left, she should have given it to you' At the mention of her money, the woman, who had been sobbing quietly, broke into loud cries:

"What shall I do? All my money for trading is gone."

But now no one was interested in her misfortune any more. Rather they all consoled Eze, and one woman offered him an orange from her bag.

"Kano, Kano," Eze heard an excited shout.

He jumped up to look through the window an: there, in the distance, he could see a great city with rows of pyramids in front of it. In the distance the white minaret and the green dome of a huge mosque rose above the flat houses.

"Well, here we are," said Ali who now joined Eze, carrying a small case. Eze was too excited to tell him about the theft of the woman's money.

"What are those pyramids?" Eze asked "Oh, they're stacks of groundnuts waiting to be carried by rail to Lagos. Beyond them you can see the city wall. It's fourteen miles long."

The train gave a great burst on its hooter and drew into Kano station. A huge crowd waited on the platform and Eze wondered how he would ever find his sister or her husband.

There was a great surge as all the passengers fought to get off the train. Ali clutched Eze's free arm and led him along the platform. Suddenly a boy about Eze's size came up shouting: "Ali, Ali. Sanu da zuwa. Sanu da zuwa."

"Ah! Adamu. It's good to see you. This is Eze. He's at the same school as me."

"Welcome, " said Adamu, who had taken his brother's case.

Eze shook his hands while Ali told his brother that he wanted him to take Eze round the city one day. Just then, Eze saw his sister advancing through the crowd.

"Eze, Eze. Welcome, Welcome.

She embraced him, and then Eze introduced Ali and Adamu to her. After greeting them she explained to Adamu where she lived and suggested that he could come round for Eze the following morning.

Ulu and her husband lived in a small bungalow in the *Sabon gari,* the stranger's quarter outside the old walled city. Adamu arrived there as promised at 10 that morning. He had a bicycle with him, and with Eze sitting on the crossbar, he cycled off to Adamu's house in the old city.

Eze marvelled at the great mud walls of the city, the huge mud gate through which they passed; the majestic palace of the Emir and the gleaming new mosque he had seen from the train. From the great square in front of the palace they cycled down a narrow alleyway till they came to a storey house whose front was decorated in green and white intricate geometric patterns.

"This is our house," said Adamu, "Come in. Mohammed has gone out, but my young brother, Daudu, is here."

Eze entered a cool, dark room with low benches round the wall, covered with leather cushions. A large round table stood in the middle, with a silver teapot and small glasses.

After Adamu had introduced Eze to his brother Daudu, who seemed to be only eight years old, he sent him out to fetch three krolas. When he returned, all three drank in silence. Then a tall lady came in. She spoke to Adamu in Hausa:

"My mother says you are welcome. She does not speak turanci - English. She would like you to eat with us."

Eze asked Adamu to thank her and tell her he would be very happy to eat in her house.

A maid then brought in two small bowls of fura de nono to cool them off after their long ride. Adamu produced a story book which they read aloud in turns until the maid returned with steaming bowls of food.

Adamu told him that the tuwo was made from millet and the *miyan taushe* with which it was served, was prepared with pumpkins.

After lunch they explored the city. At various times during the exploration, Adamu bought groundnuts and *alewa* which they ate as they went. It was not until five that afternoon that Eze got back to his sister's house. When he told her how he had eaten Hausa food at Adam's house, she insisted that Adamu should come the next day to taste her own food.

For the three weeks he was in Kano, Eze was inseparable from Adamu. He couldn't bear the thought of leaving Kano; he was so happy there.

"I wish I didn't have to leave," Eze told Adamu. "I shall miss you. It's been such fun

'Here."

"Don't worry, Eze. My father promised that I can come to Onitsha next holiday and visit him so we'll soon be together again." The next day Adamu called round to go with Eze and Ulu to the station. Mohammed had left two days before, so Eze had to travel alone. They got to the station early so that this time Eze got a seat in the com-partment.

As the train pulled slowly out of the sta-tion, Eze bravely waved goodbye to Adamu and Ulu. He blinked back the tears that came to his eyes; he felt so sad.

Chapter 9
Ohia Chang

Eze was promoted to Form III on the first day of school. As he put on the white trousers, he was now qualified to wear to school, he thought about his new position as a sen-jor boy of Prince of Peace College. Students in shorts would now respect and obey him, and he could discipline them if they broke any of the school rules.

Corporal Obi, who wore a big cloth thrown around him, was standing in front of the house, brushing his teeth with a long chewing stick.

"Good-bye, sir," Eze called to him as he set off for school.

"Where are Lawrence and Philip?" the Corporal asked, noticing how well Eze's clothes fitted him.

"They are coming, sir." "Do you know what those trousers mean?" Eze stopped and turned round.

Without waiting for an answer, the Corporal went on: "They tell all of us that you are a senior student of your school, that you have grown from a boy into a man, and that you have become responsible. We expect you therefore to be a model to every other stu-dent, especially the junior ones. You must study harder, observe your school rules more closely and give guidance to the new boys. That way you will uphold the good name of your school and help it to grow."

The calm with which the year began for Eze was ruffled one evening early in Febru-ary. He and Philip were writing their homework when Ebele screamed. They both jumped up and ran out to see what the matter was. When they learnt that it was only a cockroach that had flown into her blouse, they laughed it off and returned to their room.

"Damn," Eze hissed as he approached the table on which they had been working.

"Stop swearing. What's the matter now?"

Philip asked behind him.

"See what you have done, you oaf."

Philip's open bottle of ink lay on its side, empty. Its content had run across Eze's open workbook, staining it badly. "How can you be sure that you, yourself, didn't spill the ink when you rushed out?" Philip taunted.

"I was out of here before you, idiot, and those marks weren't there when I left."

"Two years in civilization have not taught you to keep a civil tongue in your mouth.

How true it is that even if you trained a monkey at Cambridge or Oxford, it would still return to the jungle."

"Meaning what?"

"Simply that you belong to Ohia where you originally came from."

Eze grew very angry at this reference to his background:

"Don't force me to go and make a report."

"Is it he who invites the police who wins."

"You are incorrigible... Next time, I'll fight you.""Meaning what?"

"Simply that you belong to Ohia where you originally came from."

Eze grew very angry at this reference to his background:

"Don't force me to go and make a report."

"Is it he who invites the police who wins."

"You are incorrigible ... Next time, I'll fight you." "Go easy, boy. Only mad people fight." Eze took control of himself, but Philip's constant jibes at his village background came between them and their friendship. Philip, he knew, was jealous of him because he was doing better at school, both in the class and on the playing field. But that did not excuse his constant references to Ohia as a 'bush' place, even if that is what its name meant.

Eze had even written to Wilberforce to ask him why their village should bear a name that literally meant: 'bush'.

Just before the half year holidays in July, Eze had a close encounter with a gang of robbers. Late one evening at about 10 p.m.

Corporal Obi summoned Eze, and Lawrence who was still awaiting the result of the last Cambridge School Certificate examination.

He asked them to get dressed and come with him to visit his cousin whom he had just learnt was dying. As it was late, he suggested they bring a stave or a club with them in case of danger.

They arrived at the cousin's residence, half way down Old Cemetery Road, and saw that his condition was such that he could not be moved. They fetched a doctor who attended to him and promised to return in the morning to arrange his transfer to the General Hospital. But he died half an hour after the doctor left.

Corporal Obi spent the next hour and a half consoling close relatives of the deceased and making arrangements for his burial.

When at 2 a.m. it seemed that all plans had been made, Corporal Obi decided that he and the boys would go home. They left the house and walked up Old Cemetery Road.

It was a very dark night. As they passed the cemetery itself, they heard the sound of several footsteps. They listened. The footsteps were still approaching. Yet there were no accompanying voices. They peered into the darkness, but could see no one.

"Let's take cover in the cemetery," Obi whispered to the boys urgently. "I suspect it is a gang of thieves."

They ran lightly across the road and felt their way over graves and around tomb-stones, as they went deeper and deeper into the cemetery. Eze came to a tree with a huge trunk and stood behind it, praying si-lently. After what seemed a long wait, he felt a hand on his face and froze.

"Is that you, Eze?" he heard Lawrence ask softly.

"You almost frightened the life out of me," he whispered, when he had found his voice.

A light flashed into the graveyard from "Papa is right. They are coming into the

cemetery."

"They must be ghosts or spirits, or why are they coming in here after us?"

"Spirits and ghosts don't use torches. I hope father is all right. I lost him as we ran to take cover."

As the newcomers advanced into the cem-etery, Eze and Lawrence began to hear what the voices were saying:

"What shall we do?"

"Let's move further away from the road." The torchlight flashed again in a wide arc.

Lawrence saw, by how the light shown, that the tree near which they stood had a low branch.

"You climb up, Eze, there's a low branch here. I'll help you up. Hand me your club… I'll give you my stave when you are up. If they come to this tree, hold the stave ready to strike. When you hear me fighting, you lash out with the stave. And lash out with all your might. Just make sure you don't fall off your perch "

He helped Eze up the branch and stood waiting for the visitors who were now quite close to the tree. The light flashed one more time at the foot of the tree.

"Here we are," said an authoritative voice.

"Set your loads down here and sit down.

We must work fast so that we can divide our loot and get home before the town awakes."

The men had begun obeying him even before he had finished speaking. Every single one of them - and they were about ten in number - was either bare-bodied or wore something dark.

"My father had always warned me against going into cemeteries at night when ghosts are abroad," one voice complained. "It can only bring bad luck. I don't like it."

"Sit down and shut up," another voice ordered.

"Our fathers were no fools. What they saw sitting down we can't see these days, even when we stand."

"Stop jabbering. When you start enjoying your share tomorrow, you'll forget all your old man's advice. And you won't remember me, either. Still, I'm willing to protect you against any odds tonight. So come and sit by me... That's a good boy. Lean against the tree and relax." The torchlight was now focused, away from the tree, on the loot that the thieves were sorting out into lots. Eze counted three large trunk boxes which one of the men was forcing open, four big bundles of clothes and four radio sets. From inside the boxes, they took out more women's clothes, some wads of pound notes and heaps of gold trinkets.

"Let's get out of here," the second voice pleaded, "before the ghosts show their resentment at our disturbing their peace."

"Ghosts do not exist. When a man dies, he is buried and he rots away. That's the end of him. There are no ghosts."

"Then why was a chain put round that European's grave near the road? Have you ever heard the stories of the adventures of his ghost?"

"All that is superstition, I tell you. There are no ghosts."

"We must be careful how we take women and girls on our excursions in future," another said, and the rest laughed softly Suddenly the second voice, whose idle hand had accidentally strayed to Lawrence's tennis shoes, shouted:

"Ghosts have surrounded us." he cried pitifully. "I just touched one of them."

As he rose to dash away, Lawrence's club descended on the side of his face and he crashed into his colleagues. Before the man holding the torchlight could turn round, Eze swung his stave at him, catching him on the right shoulder forcing the torch out of his hands.

"The boy is right. Make for the road," one of their colleagues cried and the robbers fled, leaving behind the torch which was still on.

Lawrence crawled to the torch, recovered it and switched it off.

"Jump down, Eze," he said. "That was well done. But we must move to another location before they return for their loot." Slowly they felt their way towards the grave with the chain around it. Arriving there, they could hear some of the robbers discussing plans to retrieve the money and trinkets that were part of the loot they had earlier abandoned."Eze, do you still remember how to hoot like an owl?"

"I'll never forget it."

"Good. Hoot and scare them some more." The sound was so natural that no one who heard it would ever suspect that it was not real.

"I am going home," one of the robbers said decisively to his friends when the owl hooted. "No one tells the deaf when a war starts." The other robbers fled with him, and when they were out of earshot, Lawrence called out:

"Father, it's all right. They've gone. Eze and I are over here." He flashed the torchlight to indicate their position.

Corporal Obi told Lawrence to go and fetch the police while he and Eze guarded the robbers' ill-gotten gain.

When Wilberforce visited the Corporal a few days later, Lawrence gave him an account of their adventure. He was very impressed with the courage of the two boys and congratulated them on thwarting the efforts of the robbers.

"I received your letter," he told Eze in the presence of everybody. "I am surprised that you had not heard of the new name for our village."

"You changed the name of your village?"

Obi asked. "Yes." "But why did you people have to do that?" Philip asked.

"We are of the same stock as the people of Ama. One day, long ago, a leopard was killed in a communal hunting expedition. When the flesh came to be divided, the man who founded our village was cheated. It was he who had delivered the death blow and that entitled him to the animal's skin. When this was denied to him, he packed up with his immediate relatives and our village."

But he didn't call it Ohia. That was a derogatory name by which the rest of the people in Ama referred to the new settlement carved out in the middle of nowhere.

When the white man came, it was first to Obodo and then to Ama, whose elders gave him the names of nearby towns and villages.

It was they who told him that our village was called: Ohia, and the white men put it on their maps. So the name stuck."

"What name did the founder of the settlement give it?" asked Obi.

"He called it: 'Abia', after the man who established our kindred."

"And what name did you change Ohia to?"

"It was resolved at the general meeting of our Improvement Union held last Boxing Day to tell the government the true story and ask that the village be recognized as: 'Abia'.

In the meantime, all citizens of the village have been ordered to refer to it as 'Abia'." Eze gave Philip a knowing look that said:

"You can't hold the name: 'Ohia' against me ever again."

Chapter 10
Adamu Visits Onitsha

"Ali has given me a message for you," Lawrence told Eze. "He says Adamu will arrive tomorrow by boat."

"Arriving by boat?" Eze looked surprised.

"His father is giving him a special treat because he came first in his class in the last promotion examination. He will travel by train to Makurdi where he will take a boat down the Benue to Lokoja. From Lokoja the boat will sail down the Niger to Onitsha."

"Did he say what time the boat will arrive?" Eze asked.

"It is estimated to arrive around 4:30 in the afternoon."

"I'll go and get permission to meet him at the waterside."

"Ali hopes you'll be able to show Adamu the city."

"But I don't know the city very well."

"Get permission from Papa for Philip to help you."

Corporal and Mrs Obi did not hesitate to grant Eze the permission he sought. They knew Adam's father and thought he was a fine gentleman.

"The cat," Mrs Obi said as Eze took his leave, "says that close contact is the spice of life, so bring your friend to the house whenever you can."

Eze and Philip were at the John Holt jetty with Adamu's father and brother, when the boat, pulling two barges, anchored. Adamu alighted and beamed when he saw the little group that had come to receive him. He bowed in greeting, first to his father and then to his brother. Then he shook hands with Eze.

"This is Philip," Eze told Adamu. "He will show both of us the city. I'm afraid I still don't know more than a tenth of it." Then to Philip he said: "This is Adamu.

I've told you so much about him."

"I feel I have known you for many years," Philip said, taking the hand Adamu stretched out to him in a firm grip: "Welcome to Onitsha."

They both saw Adamu home and promised to come back for him the next morning. Adamu was ready and waiting for them when they arrived at 9 o'clock.

"Onitsha is not as big as Kano," Eize said.

"I hope you don't mind if we walk around it."

"No, I don't mind. It will give me a better chance to see your city."

Their first stop was at the Onitsha Main Market.

"The market looks more impressive from the river," Adamu remarked. "I saw it as we sailed in yesterday and I was amazed at the number of canoes that were moored there.""It occupies 15 acres of land," Philip explained, "and almost anything you can think of is sold here. People come to it by road and river from all points of the compass." They wandered round the market for a while before they escaped from the din, along the marina. They passed the yam sellers' and wood carvers' sections; some shops and warehouses before they came to Holy Trinity Cathedral.

"I saw the spire of this church yesterday, long before I could make out the canoes. It's quite a landmark," said Adamu.

"Yes. It is the biggest church for miles around," replied Philip.

They moved on past the ferry and stopped at the suspension bridge that spanned the Nkisi just before it emptied into the Niger.

"Across the bridge, on that side, is the prison yard. We have nick-named it the:

White College, because all its inmates wear white vests and white shorts."

They turned away from the bridge and headed for the Onitsha Inland Town which Eze described as a *Birni* without ancient walls. Almost completely occupied by the

indigenes of the city, it was much quieter than the Waterside, which immigrants had transformed into a bustling business section that expanded rapidly from the market in the direction of the Inland Town. It was about noon when they left Awka Road and followed a narrow and winding street to their destination.

"Welcome to our home," Philip said to Adamu as they crossed the threshold. They both sat in the parlour while Eze went to tell Mrs Obi that Adamu had arrived."Good day, Madam," Adamu greeted Mrs

Obi as she entered the parlour.

"Welcome my son," she replied. "Eze told us how wonderful you were to him in Kano.

I hope we shall make your stay in Onitsha an equally happy one.

"Thank you, Madam," Adamu replied.

"Take Adamu to your room and play draughts while I get lunch ready."

The boys were engrossed in their game and did not know that the door had opened.

"Hello boys," Lawrence greeted them from the doorway. "You must be Ali's younger brother. You are welcome. If I were you, Eze, I would introduce Adamu to Papa before he starts wondering what mischief you are up to."

The introduction had just been completed when the boys were invited to eat lunch.

Lunch was yam fufu served with nsala soup prepared with a lot of fresh fish.

Adamu ate well before they retired to the orange tree at the back of the yard with pen-knives to pluck, peel and eat oranges.

When they took Adamu back that evening, they passed by the palace of the Obi, which was nothing to compare in size or beauty with that of the Emir of Kano.

Adamu spent most of his time in Onitsha exploring the town with Philip and Eze. They showed him where the Onitsha people once lived along the waterfront before raids by slave traders operating along the Niger forced them to found the Inland Town. They showed him Otumoye Lake and other places of interest. They also took him to Corporal Obi's farm. There, they had a meal of roast yam and enjoyed a bath and a swim in the Nkisi on their way home.

On the eve of his departure from Onitsha, Adamu called to thank Mrs Obi for her wonderful food. She had provided him with a different dish each time he came to the house.

"You are always welcome here." Mrs Obi replied.

"Now, I have this little gift for your mother," she added, pointing to a neatly packed carton. "It is some oranges and a head of unripe bananas. And this shilling is for you."

Corporal Obi then gave him five shillings.

"Thank you very much. I shall tell my parents about your kindness."

The next morning, Philip and Eze were at the motor park to bid him farewell. As the lorry in which he was travelling pulled out of the park, Adamu waved:

"Nodu mma," he shouted.

Chapter 11
School Sports

Although Eze still had a year to go before he left PPC, he was made captain of his house's athletic team. He was the fastest boy in the school at 880 yards and could give the captain of the school athletic team a good run in the 440 yards.

The inter-house athletics competition was to be held on December 15th just before the school broke up. Although they had exams early in December, Eze brought his team out daily to practice. St. Jonas' house - Eze's house - had not won the inter-house competition for four years. Eze was determined he would beat the other three houses into first place. He spent a great deal of time teaching his relay team how to change batons.

By the time sports day approached, Eze was convinced that they would beat St Patrick's house, even though its team was led by the school's athletic champion.

Sports day was a clear, cool day. The harmattan that had been blowing for three days had lifted and the air was sweet to a runner's chest. The whole school - except those who were competing - had turned out at the sports field. The masters had a row of chairs under the shade of some trees.

The first race of the day was the hundred yards. The school's athletic champion, John Anene, easily won this. But a member of Eze's team, his friend, Noah Eneli, won the long jump, and for the first five events St Jonas' and St Patrick's were running neck and neck on points. Then with the 220 yards, Anene again came first and put St Patrick's in the lead. The last race of the day was the 880 yards.

Eze was certain to win this. The school's athletic champion only ran the shorter distances, whereas Eze was a true middle-dis-tance runner. He quickly took the lead and soon he had established a twenty-yard lead which grew longer and longer. Even though there was no one to push him, Eze ran like a man possessed. When he breasted the tape a great cheer went up from the school. A minute later, while Eze was still regaining his breath, Mr Johnson announced:

"Eze Adi has broken the school record for the half-mile. His time was 21.5 seconds which beats the old record by three seconds."

A huge cheer went up from the boys for this was the first record to be broken that year.

Everywhere he went Eze received congratulations which was not good for a young head that swelled so easily. Only his friend Noah cautioned him:

"You did well, Eze. But don't get over-con-fident. If you don't win the 440 yards tomorrow, we can't win the championship.

You've got to beat Anene in that; otherwise I don't see how we can win."

"But I can't beat Anene. He is too good at 440 yards. I've never equaled his time."

"Well you can try. The house depends on you."

Eze slept soundly that night. The following morning at 8 o'clock, everyone was back on the field. The first event was the hurdles event which was won by a boy from St James' house. Then the high jump was won by St Andrew's who also took second place.

But this made little difference for those two houses were way behind St Patrick's and St Jonas'.

A hush fell over the crowd as competitors took their places for the 440 yards. Eze drew the inside lane, while Anene was unlucky to get the outside lane.

"On your marks ... Get set ..." The starter's gun exploded twice in quick succession.

"False start!" called Mr Johnson. One boy had jumped the gun. A great sigh of protest went up from the crowd

"On your marks ... Get set…BANG! This time the boys shot from their crouched position, jockeying for places on the inside trek behind Eze. Despite his great speed, Anene had some difficulty in placing himself, as Eze was right out in front. Eze strained every muscle as he pushed himself to the limits of his power.

He didn't even hear Anene creeping up on him. Indeed he was oblivious of the great cheers going up from the crowd.

"Come on, Eze. Don't let him get you," shouted the boys from St Jonas' house while those from St Patrick's, unaccustomed to seeing Anene in second place, shouted out:

"Chase him, Anene, chase him."

Anene was gaining on Eze with every stride until they were almost neck and neck.

Eze sensed his presence and, with a final spurt, hurled himself to the tape and collapsed on the track.

The crowd hesitated to cheer, for it was not at all clear who had won. Mr Johnson and the Reverend Andrew entered a deep conversation, examining their stopwatches.

The crowd waited anxiously for Mr Johnson to announce the referee's decision.

"The winner of the 440 yards race just ended is," and he paused meaningfully: "Eze Adi." A mighty roar went up from the crowd and Eze, who was now struggling to his feet, was mobbed by the boys who ran into the field to congratulate him.

He only just heard Mr Johnson declare that both he and Anene had equalled the school record of 59.2 seconds. The race had been so close that there was no difference in their times. When the boys had finished congratulating Eze, Noah came up to him: "We've as good as won the school championship. Even if we only get third place in the relay, there is no way in which we can lose. And we should, at least, come second. St Jude's and St Andrews' don't have good teams at all." At ten o'clock, after the shot put and javelin had been decided, it was clear that Noah Eneli's prediction was right. St Jonas' only had to get third place in the relay to maintain their lead and win the school championship.

Competitors for the first leg of the 440 yards relay positioned themselves at the starting line. For St Jonas', Noah

Eneli was the first runner, and Eze the last, as was Anene for St Patrick's. Eze was determined to complete a hat-trick by winning the relay and show Anene that he, Eze, was really the best athlete in the school.

Eze heard the gun go. Noah set off to a flying start and established a quick lead. Eze looked cockily at Anene.

"You see, we'll beat you," he shouted above the roar of the crowd.The second runner from St Jonas' maintained the lead established by Noah, and the third runner took his baton smartly.

"It's going to be easy," Eze thought happily.

His mind turned to the congratulations he would receive as he tensed himself for the take over. He would probably even get the cup for the best athlete of the year. As his teammate approached, he started to run so that he could pace himself alongside him as they had done so many times in practice.

But he had set off too soon, and, when he took the baton, not only had he overstepped the limits of the takeover box but he fumbled the baton and it dropped.

There was a great groan from St Jonas', followed by a huge cheer from St Patrick's as Anene flew across the tape to win the relay and the championship for his house.

Eze suddenly felt like a leper for everyone seemed to avoid him. Only Noah came up to him to commiserate with him:

"That was bad luck, Eze. But you shouldn't have been so over-confident. We only needed third place, but you weren't thinking about the house."

When the cups were given out by the Resident of Onitsha Province afterwards, Eze was given only a half-hearted cheer when he went up to get his cups for the 440 and 880 yards.

As soon as he could, Eze left for home and went to his room to read.

The next morning at school, Eze was very much a sadder and a wiser young man. The other boys in the class were all very excited because this was the day they would get their exam results and they could all go home.

When their form master, Mr Williams, came into the class, there was an anxious hush after they had greeted him.

"Well," he said, "let's see how badly you've all done."

"Bottom of the class, as usual I'm afraid, is Solomon Aguda. Where's your wisdom, young man? Your parents didn't name you wisely."

The boys didn't like Mr Williams who specialized in sarcasm at their expense. Alone of all the masters he read the results out from the bottom up: "Twenty-second is Cosmas Onoja... twenty-first is..."

By the time he reached fifth place he still had not called out Eze's name. He called fifth, then fourth, then third. Eze could not believe it. He was either going to be first or second.

"Second place: Eze Adi." The class turned enviously in his direction.

"And, first by only one mark: Innocent Okafor."

"Well done Okafor and Adi. If you keep up this level of work, we'll have you both into University College, Ibadan with no dif-ficulty."

When Noah, who had only managed sixteenth place, came up to congratulate Eze, he noticed he was much more subdued. At least, he thought to himself, Eze isn't going to let this go to his head.

Chapter 12

Eze in Trouble

On the first Sunday after the New Year, Wilberforce arrived at Corporal Obi's house early in the morning.

"I've come to spend the whole day with you," he announced after courtesies had been exchanged.

"You know you are welcome any time, any day, for as long as you may wish to stay," was Corporal Obi's reply. "Where is everybody?"

"At their household chores, I believe."

"How's Lawrence faring at his job with the BBWA?"

"He is doing well, he tells me.

Wilberforce strode round the house wishing everyone a prosperous New Year. He returned to a bottle of Gordon's gin which Obi had produced, poured himself a drink and prayed for long life and prosperity for themselves and for members of their households.

"I've been thinking," he said, when at last they were alone. He paused to decide how best to introduce the subject without giving any offence to his host. "This is Eze's last year at school. So far he has done very well. Thanks to you, your wife and your children who have contributed in no small measure to his achievements. Next year is his last year at PPC. It is important to Abia that he passes his School

Certificate Examination and possibly the entrance examination to the University College, Ibadan with distinction..."

"What are you trying to say?" Obi cut in.

"Your introduction is getting too long."

"Well, what would be your reaction if we suggested that Eze becomes a boarder when school reopens later this month?"

"No one disturbs his studies here. But 1 will endorse the suggestion if you think it will be best for Eze."

"Thank you. You do not know what pressures I suffer in my self-assigned task of developing my community. It is a thankless job, I can tell you. The Lagos branch of our Improvement Union, with a membership of only three, insisted on a boarding house for Eze. It didn't take them time to convince others at the General Meeting. I fought against it. When I saw it was no use, I insisted that they must pay the boarding fees.

And, they accepted."

"Helping one's own people isn't the easiest job there is," Corporal Obi said sympa-thetically.

Eze himself was very excited at the idea of spending his last year at PPC as a boarder.

It was not that he didn't like the life at the Obi"s. They treated him like a son. But in the evenings he only had Philip to talk to after he had finished his homework; whereas, in the boarding house, there would be Noah Eneli and many other friends.

So Eze started his final year at PPC eagerly. It was such fun that the first term seemed to slip by without his noticing it.

And soon, he was packing his box for the Easter holidays with the Obis.

When he arrived there, he made to go to his room with his box but Corporal Obi halted him:

"Put your things down here," he ordered.

Eze obeyed and the Corporal searched his haversack. After that, he demanded the key to his box. Eze opened it and Obi searched that too. His.search was thorough. At last at the bottom of the box, he found what he was looking for: a talisman.

"What is this?" he asked, holding it up.

"It's a talisman."

"Where did you get it from?"

"I got it from India."

"When was that?"

"Last month."

"What is it for?"

"It is meant to help me with my examinations."

Just then Wilberforce Ezeilo arrived.

"You could not have come at a better or rather, should I say, worse time," Obi replied to his greeting.

"Come and join us."

Wilberforce pulled up a chair and sat down.

"What's the matter?" he asked, as he saw

Eze's face.

"Abia's bright lad decided that a talisman," Obi replied, holding up the item, "will better help him to pass his exams than work-ing hard at his lessons. So, he acquired this from India."

"What!" Wilberforce cried and jumped from his chair and slapped Eze's face.

Obi tried to restrain Wilberforce:

"Violence is not the answer. It is uncalled for."

"Listen, young man," he said to Eze, how many talismans have you used in your exams these last three years? Was your performance then unsatisfactory because you didn't have one..? What made you think you needed one now?"

"I saw some students ordering them as I joined them for the fun of it."

"For the fun of it, indeed!" Wilberforce shouted.

"If in only one term as a boarder you bring back this, who knows what you will bring back after one year? I was never happy about your going to the boarding house. I've a mind to see your Principal."

"Do that and you'll get him expelled from the school," Obi warned.

"How much liberty can you give to these children who think they are wiser than their fathers?" "Not much, I dare say," Obi replied. To Eze he said: "Take your things to your room and remain there until I send for you." When he had gone the two men debated the action they should take. At last they summoned Eze before them:"You must have thought about this talisman by now," Obi said. "Did you do right by ordering it, even for fun?"

"No, sir; I'm really sorry it happened."

"How much reliance have you placed on it since you got it?"

"None at all; I've not even read the instructions on how it is used."

"Do you promise us both that this kind of thing will never happen again; that you will rely on your own ability alone, both at school and at home? Talismans are worthless bits of paper. They are no substitute for hard work and brain power. Promise you will never put faith in such rubbish again."

"I promise

"Well hold you to this promise. If you break it, you will be in very serious trouble indeed."

"Yes, sir." "You may go."

"Thank you, sirs."

After spending part of his holidays with the Obis, and part with his mother, Eze returned for the beginning of his second to last term in the school. Three weeks later, Wilberforce paid one of his regular visits to Onitsha. When he alighted at the motor park, he ran into Josephat Okonkwo, a trader from his village. They talked for a while and he turned to enter the market.

"Oh, I almost forgot," Josephat called out to him. "I saw Eze Adi at the cinema twice last week and once again this week. I wonder if the school authorities gave him permission to frequent the theatre. When does he find time to do his studies?"

"Thanks for the information. I'll see the school Principal before I go back this afternoon."

His business in the market over, Wilberforce made his way to PPC, and secured an appointment with the Principal after he had told the secretary that he had urgent business to discuss:

"How often do you allow your boarders to go to the pictures?" he asked the Principal.

"We only allow them when we know that the film that is showing will be beneficial to them," the Principal answered, somewhat surprised by the question.

"How many times did you give them permission over the last two weeks?"

"None at all, I'm certain."

"I am reliably informed that Eze Adi was at the cinema twice last week and once again this week," Wilberforce said gravely.

"That cannot be so."

"Why don't you ask him?"

Without another word, the Principal sent for him.

"Good day, sir," Eze greeted Wilberforce when he entered the Principal's office.

"How many times were you at the cinema in t

"Three,..them," the Principal answered, somewhat surprised by the question.

"How many times did you give them permission over the last two weeks?"

"None at all, I'm certain."

"I am reliably informed that Eze Adi was at the cinema twice last week and once again this week,*

"That cannot be so."

"Why don't you ask him?"

Without another word, the Principal sent for him,

"Good day, sir," Eze greeted Wilberforce when he entered the Principal's office.

"How many times were you at the cinema in the last two weeks?"

"Three times he answered after some hesitation.

"And, with whose permission?"

"I had no permission, sir."

"I am sure you didn't go alone. Who went wish you'" Eze did not answer even after the question was repeated.

"Who helped you in and out of the dormitory?" Again Eze did not answer and the Principal sent him back to his class.

"Thank you," he said to Wilberforce when Eze had gone. "If we had such cooperation from the towns-people we would be able to maintain a higher standard of discipline. I'll certainly get to the bottom of this and you will be hearing from me."

After lunch that afternoon, the Principal questioned Eze in his office for nearly an hour without extracting from him the names of his accomplices. That night at prep, word went round the senior boarders that the Principal had interrogated Eze about his cinema-going habits.

After prep the five students who were involved conferred with Eze behind the refectory. They tried to persuade Eze not to give their names to the Principal.

"Of course I won't tell him," Eze said angrily.

"Do you think I'm a sneak? And please, don't hold yourselves responsible for what may happen to me. None of you forced me into breaking the school rules. I have never told anyone before. I will not do it now." At 12:30 the next day, the Principal ordered that all classes should be suspended and all teachers and students assemble in the school hall.

At 12:45 he entered the hall, mounted the rostrum and called Eze Adi out to stand before the whole school. He spoke of Adi's death wish that his son should be educated and of

Eze's courageous struggle to go to college in fulfillment of that wish. He spoke of Wilberforce's effort to ensure that Eze completed his schooling. He recounted the contribution of Corporal Obi to Eze's progress. He even mentioned Mr Okafor's part in his education.

"Eze Adi was doing very well until he moved into the boarding house last January," he continued. "Look at him, all of you.

He looks all innocence but I tell you he is a whitened sepulchre. He has lost confidence in himself and is now seeking safety in talismans which are supposed to help him pass his exams. They have given him such false hopes that he sneaks out every now and again to go to the cinema.Eze can be nothing but a very bad influence on other students. The scriptures have taught us that if our right eye causes us to sin, we should pluck it out. But just before we do, let us see how repentant Eze Adi is for casting a shadow of doubt on the standard of discipline in this college."

He turned to Eze who stood there like granite: "I am sure you are not alone in the offences with which you are charged. Will you tell us who your accomplices are?" Eze did not seem to have heard him.

"Eze Adi," the Principal called.

"Sir."

"With whom did you go to the cinema in the last fortnight? Who aided you to leave and reenter the dormitory without being discovered?"

Eze did not answer. The Principal repeated the question several times but Eze's mouth was shut tight. He was determined that no-one would drag out the answers to the question from him.

The time was a quarter past one when the Principal turned to announce Eze's punishment to the staff and students. As he did so, Noah Eneli pushed to the front of the school:

"May I speak, sir?" he said.

"What is it?"

"I went to the cinema with Eze." A murmur ran through the whole school.

It had not subsided when another Form Four student advancing from the rear of the hall spoke up:

"I, too, went to the cinema with Eze." As three more culprits identified them-selves, the whole school seemed to hold its breath. The self-confessed culprits stood around Eze, who was now weeping unasham-edly.

Mr Johnson, Reverend Andrew and Mr Williams walked up to the rostrum and conferred with the Principal. After fifteen minutes of heated discussion, they returned to their seats. The Principal looked hard at all the faces turned towards him, cleared his throat and spoke very solemnly:

"You six owe your continued stay in this school to the intervention of the staff, especially to Mr Johnson who has watched your development right from Form I. But you must not go scot free. You will all be thrashed tomorrow morning before the whole school as an example to all the students. And if ever any of you is caught again for even the slightest offence, he will be summarily dismissed and barred from taking the School Certificate exam and the entrance exam to the University College, Ibadan."

Eze began to wonder if his troubles would ever end. Since he had become a boarder his whole world seemed to have been turned upside-down. Worst of all, as a senior boy he felt deeply humiliated by the thrashing he received in front of those to whom he should have been setting an example.

With his examinations only six months away he decided to be extra careful in everything he did. And when he went home to Abia for his rainy season vacation he called round to see Wilberforce Ezeilo.

"Sir," he addressed him. "All my troubles at PPC began when I became a boarder. Do you think I could spend my last term back at Corporal Obi's? I seemed to get more work done there, And, I really do want to go to University College if I can."

Wilberforce considered his request for some time before he spoke. After all, the Principal might not agree, and members of the Improvement Union would not easily change their minds. But Wilberforce, him-self, believed Eze's best hope of keeping out of trouble would be to return to Corporal Obi's house.

"I'll see what I can do," said Wilberforce, without any commitment. But as Wilberforce rarely failed in anything he set out to do, before Eze returned to Onitsha, all was arranged. The Principal agreed to the plan. The Improvement Union had finally been persuaded by the argument that this was the only hope for them to be the first village in the area to send a son to the University College at Ibadan.

From October to December Eze worked like a man possessed. Philip now found it very boring sharing his room, for Eze had time to spare only for his books.

In December, Eze together with Noah Eneli and forty other boys spent a week shut up in the musty School Assembly Hall,where Eze had so recently been beaten, writing their examinations. But when they were finished, there was over four months to wait for the result.

While he was waiting for his results, Eze went home to stay with his mother. He was very bored in the village, and as often as possible he would go to Onitsha to stay with the Obis who as usual welcomed him as a son. Philip, too, was waiting for his results and the two of them spent hours discussing how well or badly they did in particular pa-pers, and what grade they might get.

It was during a visit to the Obis in May that Eze received a message that he was to see the Principal of Prince of Peace College as soon as possible. Eze knew it must be something to do with his examinations. But surely if he had passed, they would have just sent him a letter. So fearing the worst, he put on his cleanest shirt and best-pressed trousers and set off for his old college.

When he entered the Principal's Office, the Principal came from behind his desk and walked towards Eze smiling.

"Congratulations, young man," he said, as he shook Eze's surprised hand. "You've passed so well in your Cambridge

School Certificate Examination that I have no doubt you'll get admission to Ibadan. And I'm arranging for you to sit the University College entrance exam."

Eze could not say a word; he was too overcome by the good news.

The Principal continued: "I began to wonder whether you would ever make it when you began to have so many problems last year. But it seems you took my warning to heart. And, I and the school are very proud of you."

But Eze's mind was far away, thinking of the little boy he once was, setting off by foot to the little village school at Ama. He thought of all those who had helped him get where he was - his mother who respected her husband's dying wish, Mr Okafor, Wilberforce and Corporal Obi. And finally, the three masters who had saved him from expulsion. He could not feel proud of him-self, but only of those who had had such faith in him.